It's a Gas!

Other titles in the Sidesplitters series you might enjoy:

Illustrated by
Martin Chatterton and Jane Eccles

MACMILLAN CHILDREN'S BOOKS

First published 2012 by Macmillan Children's Books
a division of Macmillan Publishers Limited
20 New Wharf Road, London N1 9RR
Basingstoke and Oxford
Associated companies throughout the world
www.panmacmillan.com

ISBN 978-1-4472-0734-4

1 3 5 7 9 8 6 4 2

A CIP catalogue record for this book is available from
the British Library.

Typeset by Nigel Hazle
Printed and bound by CPI Group (UK) Ltd, Croydon CR0 4YY

How many farts does it take to make a stink bomb?

A phew.

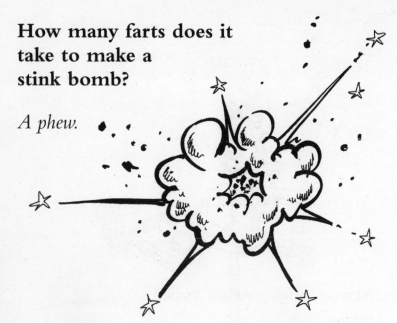

A boy walks into a shop with a big pile of dog poo in his hand. He looks at the shopkeeper and says, 'Phew, look at that. And to think I nearly stepped in it!'

Why did Tigger look in the toilet?

He was searching for Pooh.

Man: I'd like some toilet paper, please.

Woman: What colour would you like?

Man: Just give me white, I'll colour it myself!

3

Why did the toilet paper roll down the hill?

Because it wanted to get to the bottom.

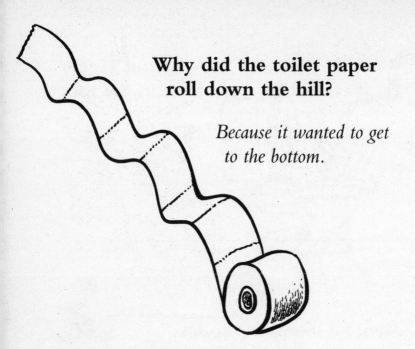

What do you call a fairy that hasn't washed?

Stinkerbell.

What do you get if you walk under a cow?

A pat on the head.

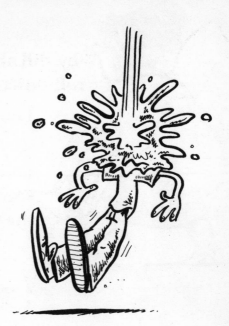

Why does Batman wear his Y-fronts outside his trousers?

To keep them clean.

Knock, knock!
Who's there?
Donna.
Donna who?
Donna sit there, someone peed on the seat!

What goes ho ho, plop plop?

Santa Claus on the toilet.

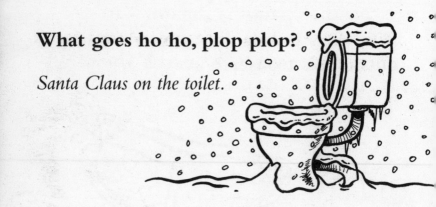

Tom had to go to the doctor because every time he tried to speak he farted.

'You must (fffaaaart) help me, Doctor, it's so (whwhhifflleeee) embarrassing. The only good thing (pffllpffll) is that my farts (ssspphhhwhee) don't smell.'

'Hmmm,' said the doctor. 'I will have to send you to a specialist.'

'Will that be (fffaaaart) a bottom specialist or a (pffllpfll) surgeon?' asked Tom.

'Neither,' said the doctor. 'I'm sending you to a nose specialist. There's something very wrong with yours!'

**What do you get
if you cross a
skunk with a
dog?**

Rid of the dog.

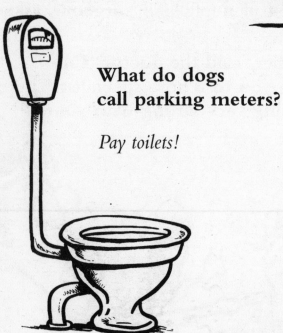

**What do dogs
call parking meters?**

Pay toilets!

What's big and grey and has odour problems?

A smellyphant.

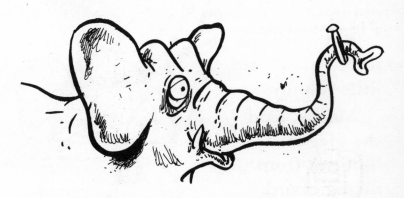

What's brown and sounds like a bell?

Dung.

Little Johnny was approached by the lifeguard at the public swimming pool.

'You're not allowed to pee in the pool,' said the lifeguard. 'I'm going to report you.'

'But everyone pees in the pool,' said little Johnny.

'Maybe,' said the lifeguard, 'but not from the diving board.'

What's invisible and smells like bananas?

Monkey farts.

What did the first mate see in the spaceship's toilet?

The captain's log.

What do you call a smelly Teletubby?

Stinky Winky.

What do cannibals do at a wedding?

Toast the bride and groom.

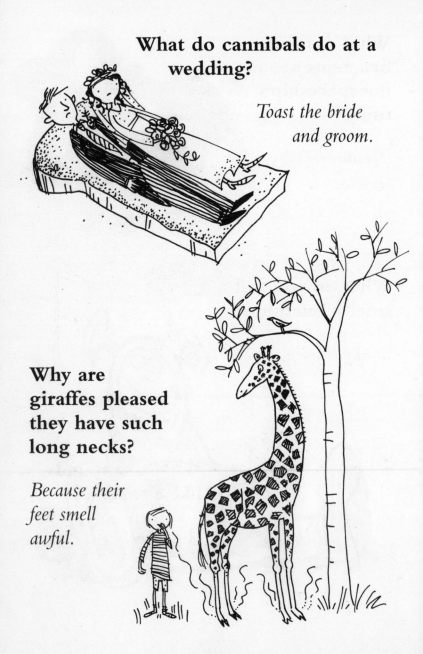

Why are giraffes pleased they have such long necks?

Because their feet smell awful.

**What can access
cyberspace
but is very
smelly?**

*A hum
computer.*

**What nut sounds
like a sneeze?**

A cashew.

'What's the difference between dog poo and chocolate?'

'I don't know.'

'In that case, don't ever buy me chocolate.'

What kind of peas are brown?

Poopeas.

What's green and smelly?

The Incredible Hulk when he farts.

What's the sharpest thing in the world?

A fart. It goes through your trousers and doesn't even leave a hole.

What's huge, green, and sits around moaning all day?

The Incredible Sulk.

Why did Frankenstein's monster get indigestion?

He bolted down his food.

Which monster makes strange noises in its throat?

A gargoyle.

What goes ha, ha, ha, crash?

An alien laughing his head off.

A belch is just one gust of wind
That cometh from the heart,
But should it take the downward route
It turns into a fart.

What's wet, brown, and smells like peanuts?

Elephant puke.

What do you get if you cross an elephant with a budgie?

A bird with a very dirty cage.

Why was the computer nut away from school?

He'd caught a computer bug.

First man: My dog's got no nose.

Second man: How does he smell?

First man: Awful.

What vegetable can you find in a toilet?

A leek.

What's a dirty book?

One that's been dropped in the toilet.

What smells, runs all day, and lies around at night with its tongue hanging out?

A pair of old trainers.

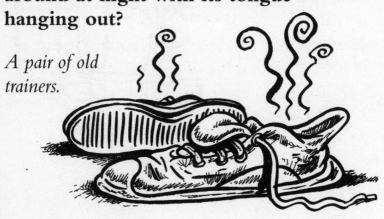

What's the difference between school lunches and horse poo?

School lunches are usually cold.

There was a young lady from Philly
Who cooked a large pot of chilli.
She ate the whole lot
Straight from the pot,
And ran to the loo in a jiffy!

Stacey: I've just bought a pig.

Tracey: Where are you going to keep it?

Stacey: In the kitchen.

Tracey: But what about all the smell and mess?

Stacey: The pig will just have to get used to it!

What do you get if you cross a skunk with an owl?

Something that smells but doesn't give a hoot!

How many skunks does it take to raise a big stink?

A phew.

What do you get if you eat baked beans and onions?

Tear gas.

What did the skunk say when the wind changed direction?

'It's all coming back to me now.'

Three very thirsty men were trekking through the desert and came across a magician. The magician was standing at the top of a slide. The magician said, 'You may each go down the slide, asking for a drink. When you reach the bottom, you will land in a huge refreshing pool of the drink you have asked for.'

The first man went down and yelled, 'Lemonaaaaade!'

The second man went down and yelled, 'Coooooke!'

The third man went down and yelled, 'Wheee-eeeeee!'

Why did the boy take toilet paper to the birthday party?

Because he was a party pooper.

What's green and smells?

An alien's nose.

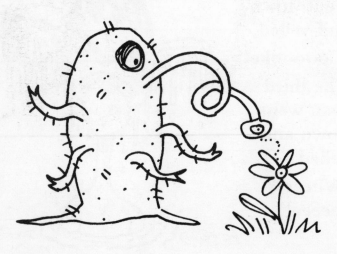

What's the difference between a huge, ugly, smelly monster and a bag of sweets?

People like sweets.

Birdie, birdie in the sky
Dropped some white stuff in my eye.
I'm a big girl, I won't cry.
I'm just glad that cows don't fly.

Did you hear the joke about the fart?

You don't want to. It stinks!

What does the Queen do if she breaks wind?

She issues a royal pardon.

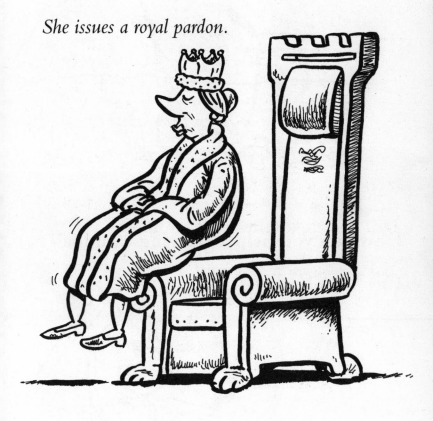

How many rotten eggs were in the omelette?

A phew!

How can you help a starving cannibal?

Give him a hand.

Knock, knock!
Who's there?
Butter.
Butter who?
Butter be quick, I need the loo!

Why wouldn't the skeleton go bungee jumping?

Because he didn't have the guts.

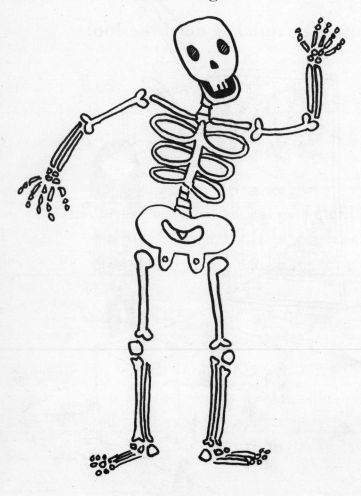

If you sprinkle when you tinkle,
Please be sweet and wipe
the seat.

A little boy asked his teacher if he
could go to the toilet.

'Only if you can recite the alphabet,'
said the teacher.

'OK,' said the boy. 'ABCDEFGHI-
JKLMNOQRSTUVWXYZ.'

'Where's the P?' asked the
teacher.

'Running down my
leg,' said the boy.

How can you stop a
skunk from smelling?

Put a peg on its nose.

Pardon me for being so rude,
It was not me, it was my food.
It just popped up to say hello,
And now it's gone back down below.

What's the last thing to go through a fly's mind when he hits the windscreen?

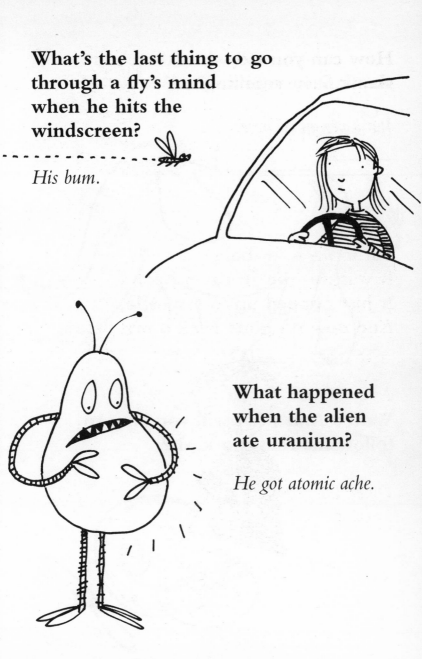

His bum.

What happened when the alien ate uranium?

He got atomic ache.

How can you tell when there's an elephant in your custard?

It's very lumpy.

Waiter: And what will you have to follow the roast pork, sir?

Diner: Indigestion, I expect.

Did you hear the one about the constipated mathematician? He worked it out with a pencil!

Melissa: Do you know anyone who has been on the TV?

Jason: My brother did once but he uses the toilet now.

Charlie: What do you clean your top teeth with?

Mum: A toothbrush and toothpaste.

Charlie: And your bottom?

Mum: The same.

Charlie: Oh, gross! I use toilet paper.

How can you tell when a gorilla's been in the fridge?

There are hairs in the butter.

Why did the alien have a bath?

So he could make a clean getaway.

What do you call a woman with two lavatories on her head?

Lulu.

Why do doctors and nurses wear masks?

So that if they make a mistake, the patient won't know who did it.

An elderly woman is riding in a lift in a very luxurious hotel when a young, beautiful woman gets in, smelling of expensive perfume. She turns to the old woman and says snootily, 'It's called Romance, and it costs thirty pounds a bottle.'
Then another young, beautiful woman smelling of perfume gets in and says, also very snootily, 'Eternal, sixty pounds a bottle.'

Around three floors later the elderly
woman has reached her destination
and is about to leave the lift. She turns
round, looks right into the eyes of
both of the young women, farts loudly,
and says, 'Broccoli – two pounds a
kilogram!'

How does a cannibal greet a guest?

'Pleased to eat you.'

Why is it foolish to upset a cannibal?

You might find yourself in hot water.

**What do you get
if you cross a
fish with a pig?**

Wet and dirty.

**What's special about a birthday cake
made with baked beans?**

*It's the only cake that can blow out
its own candles.*

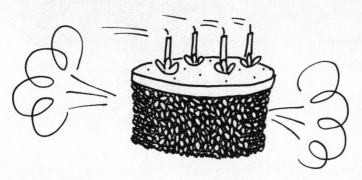

I sat next to a duchess
at tea.
   It was just as I
      feared it would be.
      Her rumbling
         abdominal
      Was simply
         phenomenal,
And everyone
thought it was me.

I'm going to have
to let one rip.
Do you mind?

*Not if you don't
mind when I
throw up.*

What's brown, smelly, and sits on a piano stool?

Beethoven's last movement.

What do you do if you give an elephant chilli?

Get out of the way.

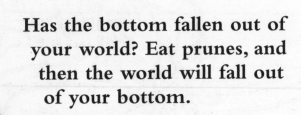

Has the bottom fallen out of your world? Eat prunes, and then the world will fall out of your bottom.

Knock, knock!
Who's there?
Ivan.
Ivan who?
Ivan itchy bottom.

What's the difference between a toilet brush and a biscuit?

You can't dip a toilet brush in your hot chocolate!

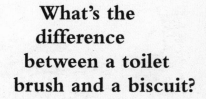

49

What's the difference between a Brussels sprout and a bogey?

You can't get a kid to eat Brussels sprouts.

Why was the stable boy so busy?

Because his work kept piling up!

What's worse than taking a bite of your apple and finding a worm?

Finding half a worm.

Why can't you hear a pterodactyl go to the toilet?

Because it has a silent 'p'.

'Doctor, Doctor, I'm going bald. Do you have anything to cure it?'

'Yes, put one pound of horse poo on your head every morning.'

'And will that cure me?'

'No, but no one will come close enough to see that you don't have any hair!'

THE WORLD'S
BIGGEST BOGEY

STEVE HARTLEY

TO THE MANAGER
The Great Big Book
of World Records
London

Dear Sir,
I have been collecting
bogeys from my nose for the
last two years.
I have stuck them all together
to make one enormous bogey. It
measures 5.3 cm in diameter and
weighs 3.6 grams. Is this a record?

Yours faithfully,

Danny Baker

(Aged nine and a bit)

WARNING!
THIS STORY
MAY CONTAIN
SILLINESS

Join Danny as he attempts to smash a
load of revolting records, including:

LOUDEST TRUMP!
CHEESIEST FEET!
NITTIEST SCALP!

ANDY GRIFFITHS & TERRY DENTON

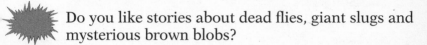

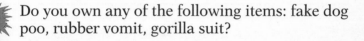

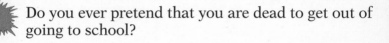

IS THIS THE RIGHT BOOK FOR YOU?
TAKE THIS TEST TO FIND OUT.

Do you like stories about dead flies, giant slugs and mysterious brown blobs?

Do you ever pretend that you are dead to get out of going to school?

Do you own any of the following items: fake dog poo, rubber vomit, gorilla suit?

Do you do any – or all – of the following: pick your nose, talk in burps or wee in swimming pools?

Do you wish that you knew the most disgusting words in the world?

SCORE ONE POINT FOR EACH 'YES' ANSWER

3–5   You are completely and utterly disgusting.
        You will love this book.

1–2   You are fairly disgusting.
        You will love this book.

0   You are a disgusting liar.
        You will love this book.

A selected list of titles available from Macmillan Children's Books

The prices shown below are correct at the time of going to press. However, Macmillan Publishers reserves the right to show new retail prices on covers, which may differ from those previously advertised.

Sidesplitters

A Joke a Day	978-0-330-51304-3	£3.99
Belly Laughs	978-0-753-41584-9	£2.99
Champion Crack-ups	978-1-4472-0839-6	£3.99
Ha! Ha! Ha!	978-0-230-75860-5	£3.99
Intergalactic!	978-0-330-51019-6	£3.99

All Pan Macmillan titles can be ordered from our website, www.panmacmillan.com, or from your local bookshop and are also available by post from:

Bookpost, PO Box 29, Douglas, Isle of Man IM99 1BQ
Credit cards accepted. For details:
Telephone: 01624 677237
Fax: 01624 670923
Email: bookshop@enterprise.net
www.bookpost.co.uk

Free postage and packing in the United Kingdom